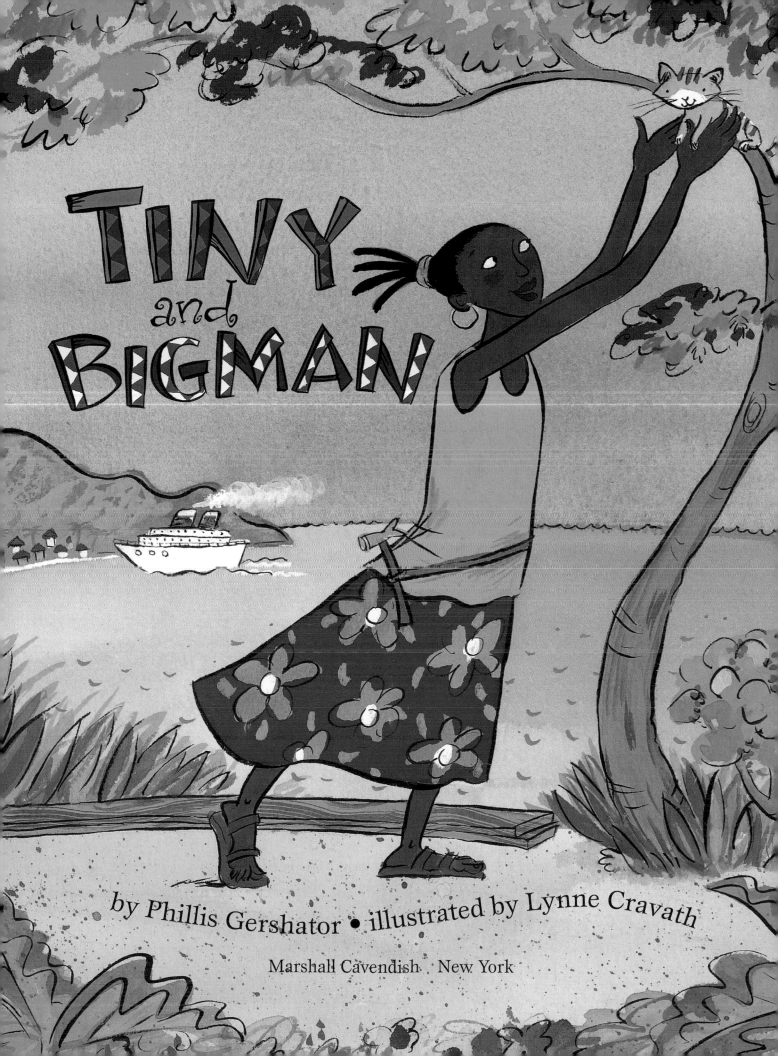

# TINY
## and
# BIGMAN

by Phillis Gershator • illustrated by Lynne Cravath

Marshall Cavendish  New York

Marshall Cavendish, 99 White Plains Road, Tarrytown, NY 10591

The text of this book is set in 14 point Esprit.
The illustrations are rendered in watercolor.
Printed in Italy
1  3  5  6  4  2

Library of Congress Cataloging-in-Publication data
Gershator, Phillis.
Tiny and Bigman / by Phillis Gershator ; illustrated by Lynne Cravath
Summary: On an island in the West Indies, a big, strong woman with a booming voice meets a weak,
nearly deaf man, they fall in love and expect a baby and a hurricane at the same time.
ISBN 0-7614-5044-0
[1. Hurricanes—Fiction. 2. West Indies—Fiction. 3. Tall tales.] I. Cravath, Lynne Woodcock, ill. II. Title.
PZ7.G316Ti   1999      [E] — dc21      98-8833      CIP      AC

To my sister, Marina — P.G.

To Jay, who is always
        properly grateful — L.C.

Miss Tiny lived on a green and rocky island in the West Indies. Miss Tiny was super friendly and always ready to offer a helping hand. She was pretty, too—soft brown skin and flashing almond eyes and a smile that made you smile back. But she didn't have a man friend to court her and take her to be his wife. "Why not?" you ask.

This is why.

Tiny had a booming voice. Not only that, she was big and strong. She could do what nobody else could do and do it twice as fast. She could tell them so, too, twice as loud.

If Tiny came across a man struggling with a heavy piece of blue bit, she'd say, "You worried about that itty-bitty stone?

"Don't let it vex you.

"I can carry it. No problem."

She'd lift up the stone like it was a pebble and place it where it had to go.

You'd think that man would be grateful and grab Miss Tiny and kiss, kiss, kiss her on her soft brown cheek. Noooo. He'd grumble and mumble a whispery "Thanks."

If a man was chopping a bit of sugarcane to sell by the roadside and the heat was wearing him down, Tiny would like as not come along and give him a break. "It too hot for you, man? Don't let it vex you. I can cut a little cane. No problem."

Tiny didn't even need a machete! She swung a sickle through the tough cane like it was tender grass. And before she could work up a thirst, the work was done.

You'd think that man would be grateful and grab Miss Tiny and kiss, kiss, kiss her on her soft brown cheek. Noooo. He'd grumble and mumble a whispery "Thanks."

When she came upon a man digging a worrisome foundation, Tiny couldn't help but help. "You having trouble reaching the four corners? Don't let it vex you. I have a minute to shovel some dirt. No problem."

Tiny jabbed the shovel into the nasty clay soil like it was rice pudding. She cut four corners neat as the edges of a page.

You'd think that man would be grateful and grab Miss Tiny and kiss, kiss, kiss her on her soft brown cheek. Noooo. He'd grumble and mumble a whispery "Thanks."

When it came time to build a deep-water port for their green and rocky island, everybody said, " We can't do it ourselves. We'll have to rent lots of big machinery and hire outsiders."

Tiny said, "I can shovel dirt. Why can't I shovel sand? No problem."

And she got a mask and a long, long snorkel and an even longer shovel, and set to work. The sand and rocks fairly flew. Lumpy piles settled down into those nearby islands we call cays. She dug so deep, even the biggest ships could slide into port without a hitch.

For her trouble, she got to keep the pieces of eight she found in the sand, left over from old-time pirate days, but not one little kiss.

Why not? Because the men all said, "Who likes a woman stronger than man? Make him look weak, weak, weak, that's what."

One day, a new fellow appeared on the scene. Speaking of weak, he was a skinny thing, with not a muscle in sight. *Everybody's* got skin and bones and all those other bodily parts, unless they're spirits without a body, of course. But with this skinny fellow, there were no muscles to be seen among the skin and bones.

The other men grinned. One said, "Wait till that skinny man meets Tiny. When she talks, he'll think a hurricane blew through his ears." Another laughed and laughed. "Tiny gives that skinny man a hug, he'll mash-up like a ripe banana!"

The skinny fellow, who went by the name of Mr. Bigman, was planning to build himself a house and plant a garden. He bought a prime piece of property by the shore.

Poor Mr. Bigman. He was so weak, he could barely hammer a nail. When Tiny saw him trying to build a house, she said, " I see you're having trouble constructing a shelter. Don't be vexed."

And she helped him haul lumber and cut it and hammer it together. When the frame of the house was all in place, she topped it off with a tin roof. Mr. Bigman had a house in one day! He was so grateful, he grabbed Miss Tiny and gave her a big hug and kiss.

"You're the strongest, most capable woman I ever met, Miss Tiny.
And you talk so nice and clear, not like most people do, grumbling and
mumbling under their breath."

"Well, that's sweet of you to say, Mr. Bigman," she boomed.

"Yes, indeed, I hear you fine," he said. " I'm a little deaf you see. Boxed
on the ears one time too many when I was a boy. Finally used my wits and
ran away to school before I got completely deaf. But if you speak up, I can
hear everything you say."

"I'll do that, Mr. Bigman," she yelled.

"Now, Miss Tiny, I hope you won't stay away just because the house is done."

So Tiny boomed into his ear, "I'll come again and help you plant your garden. No problem."

Mr. Bigman was so weak he could barely move a stone, let alone
break up the ground.

While Tiny cleared and dug up the ground like she was some kind of
bulldozer, Bigman cooked up a pot of goat stew with onions and tomatoes.
He baked a coconut tart and chilled two tall glasses of sweet hibiscus tea.
Tiny finished working just in time for lunch.

"You're a good cook, Mr. Bigman. You set a fine table," she told him.

"Thank you, Miss Tiny, but this is nothing. Wait until you taste my
Christmas cake, chock full of fruit."

The other men stopped laughing when they saw how well Tiny and Bigman got on. Tiny was showing off her strength, painting and weeding and fixing. But Bigman didn't seem to mind. He was doing just fine. He was properly grateful, too, kissing Miss Tiny all day long on her soft brown cheek and once in a while on her pretty red lips.

He didn't look mash-up at all. His smile was always answering Tiny's smile, and before long they were smiling together before the preacher.

Tiny yelled, "I do," and Bigman said, "Preacher's mumbling, Tiny. Just tell me when to say the words."

Tiny moved into the house by the shore. She puttered around outside, while Bigman invested her pieces of eight and kept the accounts.

Living on the shore, they enjoyed a good breeze all year long, but sometimes big winds and heavy clouds circled over the Atlantic Ocean and headed towards the green and rocky islands in the Caribbean Sea. When a storm threatened to come too close, Tiny took a deep breath and blew it back out to sea.

One afternoon, Tiny had a happy announcement to make:
"Baby coming soon, Bigman!"

Tiny puffed up her cheeks, took a deep, deep breath, and blew but that hurricane kept coming. It spun across the sea and hurled the waves high up onto the beach.

Tiny blew even harder, with a loud whistle and a wheeze, but the hurricane kept coming. It chewed up leaves into thick, green soup, tore branches off trees, and yanked up their trunks by the roots.

Tiny blew harder still, her lungs near to bursting, but the hurricane kept coming. It slammed the house from every direction, battering at it like a demolition crew gone *bazadee*.

Tiny blew hard, hard, hard. But even Tiny was no match for a 200 mile an hour wind.

She shouted over the din, "I don't give up easily, Bigman. It's a vexing storm, for true, and a heap of trouble. But I'm not about to let our baby go without a roof over its head!"

Tiny got a grip on the beams and rafters and pulled with all her might. She held down the roof tight, tight, tight. The roof stayed on and the rain stayed out, and the baby was born in a nice, dry house.

Before long, Tiny and Bigman has a passel of young ones, who loved to hear the story of Tiny and Bigman—and Hurricane Baby.

**Note:**
**Bazadee:** crazy, confused, from the French *abasourdir*.
**Blue bit:** one name for a hard island rock of volcanic origin (blue-gray felsite).
**Hibiscus tea:** To make it, steep red hibiscus flowers in boiling water. Strain to remove flowers and any stray ants. The liquid will be dark and cloudy. Add fresh squeezed lime juice. Like magic, the tea will turn clear and pink. Sweeten to taste and serve hot or cold.